This book belongs to:

....

....

....

To my beautiful girl ~
Sally
With special thanks to dearest
family and friends, and all who
helped this story along.

B‖F‖&‖F

BRUBAKER, FORD & FRIENDS

AN IMPRINT OF THE TEMPLAR COMPANY LIMITED

First published in the UK simultaneously in
hardback and paperback in 2013
by Templar Publishing,
Deepdene Lodge, Deepdene Avenue,
Dorking, Surrey, RH5 4AT, UK

www.templarco.co.uk

Copyright © 2013 by Ophelia Redpath

First edition

ISBN 978-1-84877-266-3 (hardback)
ISBN 978-1-84877-867-2 (paperback)

Printed in China

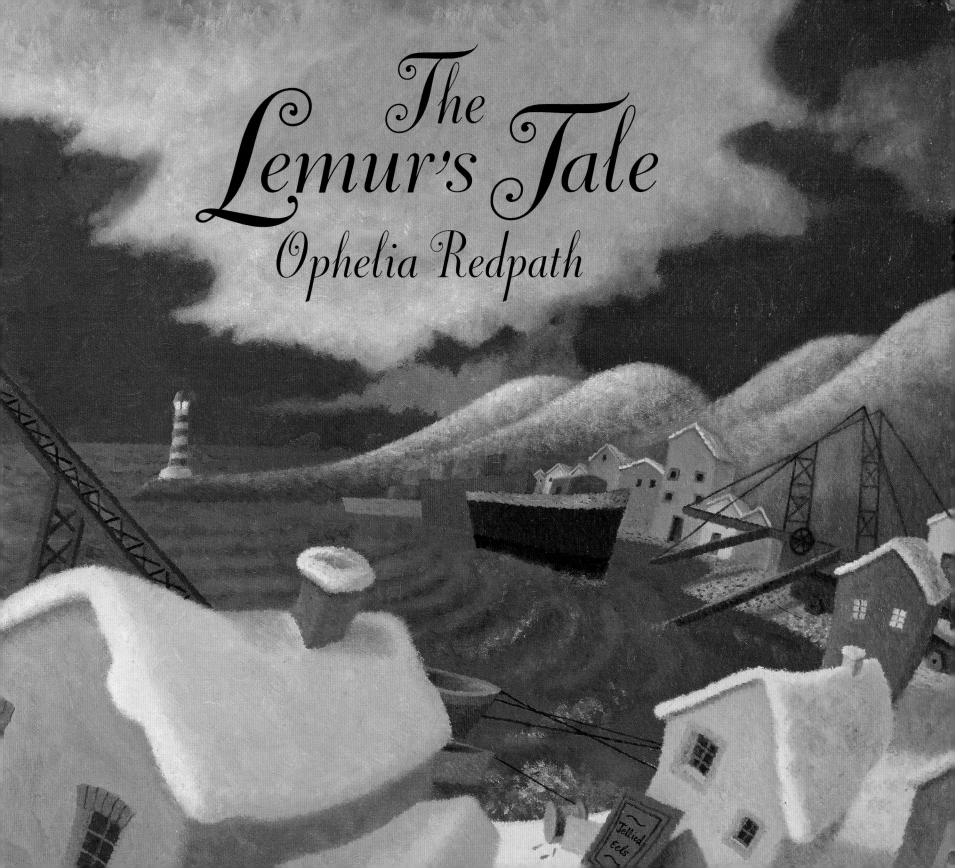

The Lemur's Tale
Ophelia Redpath

In a small cage on a big ship in a busy, busy port sat a baby lemur, far from his home in Madagascar.

He was lonely without his family, bored in his cage, frightened of the thieves who had stolen him, and shocked by the cold, cold winter.

At night, his dreams were of hot countries, faraway forests and birds of paradise. By day, he shivered in the icy winds and planned his escape.

One evening his cage was left open and he seized his chance.

He raced down the gangplank and sped along the harbour

towards the town, searching for somewhere safe.

Dashing up a tree and darting over rooftops,

he was drawn to a window, glowing with light,

of a cosy little house across a narrow street.

The baby lemur pressed his nose to the glass. Inside, lush green plants grew everywhere. They reminded him of home.

Up, up, up he scrambled until he reached a damp, dark chimney. Down, down, down he scuttled and landed in an empty fireplace.

There he waited until all was quiet.

Slowly, silently, he crept
out to find food.

He burrowed under
a pile of newspapers,
rummaged inside
a silken hat, nibbled
at a tasty orchid,
and squeezed under
the larder door.

There he began a long
and sticky feast.

When he was full, he
hid away in a secret
spot and sank into
a deep sleep.

At breakfast, Mrs Laruby poured a smidgen of her favourite treat, dandelion syrup, into her coffee.

"Gracious, dearest!" she said to her husband. "This jug was quite full yesterday! Have you been squiffling my dandelion syrup?"

"Dandelion? Squiffling? *Me*?" gasped Mr Laruby.

"Well... It must have been someone!" sniffed his wife.

Slowly, they turned to look at their daughter, Lara.

"It wasn't me!" said Lara. She couldn't think of anything more horrible than her mother's dandelion syrup.

After lunch, Mr Laruby asked his wife to bring

him *his* favourite treat, a sweet marzipan pig.

Mrs Laruby searched the larder but could

find nothing but a curly pink tail.

"My pig!" spluttered Mr Laruby. "Oh, wife!

Explain yourself!"

"Oh, husband! A woman with a waist as trim

as mine would never go *near* a marzipan pig!"

They turned to look at Lara.

"I don't like marzipan!" she protested.

After supper, Mr Laruby
went to water his plants.

Something was wrong.

"My orchid!" he bellowed.
"What has happened to
my beautiful orchid?"

Mrs Laruby hurried
to his side.

"What *has* that girl been
up to now?" she gasped.

"IT WASN'T ME!"
screamed Lara.

"Up to your
bedroom at
once!" ordered
Mrs Laruby.

"AT ONCE!"
echoed Mr Laruby.

Lara flew up the stairs, threw open her door, dived onto her bed...

"I do worry about Lara," whispered Mrs Laruby. "Perhaps she's a little lonely."

Mr Laruby scratched his head and polished his magnifying glass.

and cried her eyes out.

Later, when the Larubys were snoring in their beds, the lemur crept out.

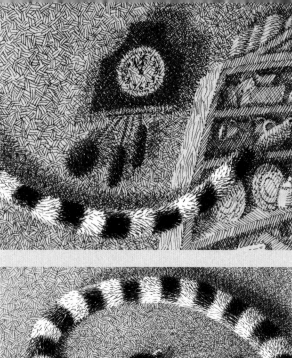

He inspected inks in the study, played with powder in the bathroom, and borrowed a brush from Mrs Laruby's dressing table.

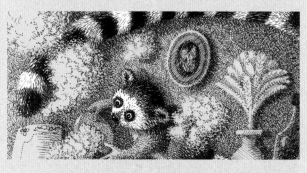

Then, slowly, silently, he glided into Lara's bedroom. There, with his beautiful tail, he swept a tear from the sleeping girl's cheek.

That night, Lara dreamt of hot countries, faraway forests and birds of paradise.

Once more, the lemur retired to his hiding place.

The next morning, Mr Laruby announced

he felt like tea instead of coffee.

Mrs Laruby went pink with excitement.

"We haven't had tea for ages!" she laughed.

"I'll clean out the pot." She reached for the

teapot on top of the dresser. It felt very heavy.

When she took off the lid, she nearly fainted.

"Heavens! Do look, my love! There's something here."

Mr Laruby hurried over and stared inside.

"What is *that*?" asked his wife.

Mr Laruby turned pale. "*That*, my dear woman," he hissed through gritted teeth, "*was* a very splendid, very exquisite, remarkably rare orchid from Madagascar." He sat down with a thump.

"No, dear! That furry thing!" insisted Mrs Laruby.

Mr Laruby took a closer look. "Utterly odd!" he mused. "That's a ring-tailed lemur."

The house went silent.

Slowly, Mrs Laruby turned to face her daughter.

"I'm so sorry for not believing you, darling," she whispered tenderly.

Lara looked curiously at the teapot. As she did so, the lemur woke up, sprang into her arms, and because he was so very shy, he nestled deep into the folds of her dress.

"Well, fancy!" laughed
Mr Laruby.

"Can he stay?" asked
Lara.

"Of course! We'll
call him Earl Grey!"
proclaimed Mr Laruby.

"And because he is so
very far away from
home, he can stay
as long as he likes,"
whispered Mrs Laruby,
hugging Lara.

And that is what he did.

To this day, Earl Grey still appears

at Lara's bedside for stories of

hot countries, faraway forests

and birds of paradise.

Just as Lara's dreams begin, he retires

to his teapot and sleeps soundly.

No one can explain
how he manages to
put the lid on.

LIFE OF BARNACLES

HERBS

W. know tha
retam
ago.

THE VARIATION OF ANIMALS AND
PLANTS UNDER DOMESTICATION

it allow

Strong a is the fo
the incessant ap
These, whether
the most tr
shade of c
lock of
the b

TOFF
ANIS